For the ones I love.
David Bedford

For Oliver, William, Lara, George and Louis. Five very grand children.
John Butler

First published in Great Britain in 2016
by Boxer Books Limited.
www.boxerbooks.com
Boxer® is a registered trademark of Boxer Books Limited.

The illustrations were prepared in watercolour.
The text is set in Adobe Garamond Pro.

ISBN 978-1-910126-07-3

1 3 5 7 9 10 8 6 4 2

Printed in China

All of our papers are sourced from managed forests and renewable resources.

Love Is a Magical Feeling

by David Bedford

illustrated by John Butler

Boxer Books

Love is a magical feeling
when you wake up and see a big smile,
bright, shining eyes and arms reaching out
then having a hug for a while.

Love feels like bumps down to breakfast

and using your teddy-bear spoon,

then letting your mum scrub and wipe your face clean

while you hum a hummy-hum tune.

is that going-out feeling

your feet feel all warm

r boots . . .

and you're stamping and stomping

and hopping about . . .

and making some really loud hoots.

Love is like picnics in meadows

when a butterfly sits on your nose . . .

and you eat up all of your favourite things
while a ladybird tickles your toes.

Love is that tingly feeling

when you've been chased away by a storm . . .

and you find a place

to keep you both dry

then cuddle up close to keep warm.

And love is that so happy feeling
when things that went wrong
are put right . . .

and seeing how many stars you can count

before telling the moon a 'Goodnight!'

Love feels like sharing a story,
all tucked up and snug in your bed,
then sinking down deep in your pillow
and resting your so-sleepy head.

And love is that magical feeling

that even when you're fast asleep . . .

you can feel the love all around you,

a love that is all yours to keep.